KT-572-105
700041700531

BIG
Bouncy
Bed

To Ursula, who likes bouncing — J.J.

For Harry Llewellyn Williams — A.R.

ORCHARD BOOKS

338 Euston Road, London NW1 3BH

Orchard Books Australia

Level 17/207 Kent Street, Sydney, NSW 2000

First published in 2014 by Orchard Books

ISBN 978 1 40830 543 0

Text © Julia Jarman 2014

Illustrations © Adrian Reynolds 2014

The rights of Julia Jarman to be identified as the author and of Adrian Reynolds
to be identified as the illustrator of this work have been asserted by them in
accordance with the Copyright, Designs and Patents Act, 1988.

A CIP catalogue record for this book is available from the British Library.

1 3 5 7 9 10 8 6 4 2

Printed in China

Orchard Books is a division of Hachette Children's Books,

an Hachette UK company.

www.hachette.co.uk

JULIA JARMAN & ADRIAN REYNOLDS

BIG Bouncy Bed

ORCHARD

Ben and Bella on the big bouncy bed.

Boing!
Boing!
Boing!
Boing!

Mind your head!
Springs go squeak.
Bed goes creak.

But who's that going, "Eek-eek-eek"?

"Hello, kids, is there room for me?"

"Oh yes, Mouse. Come up and see!"

Mouse leaps on and jumps up high.

Covers slip and pillows fly!

Mouse, Ben and Bella on the big bouncy bed.

Boing!

Boing!

Boing!

Boing!

Mind your head!

Springs go squeak.
Bed goes creak.

Mouse is flying —
"Eek-eek-eek!"

Covers slip and pillows fly!

"Who's down there?" Bella cries.

"Hi there, kids! Can I bounce too?"

"Come on up, Kangaroo!"

Kanga leaps. **What a bound!**
Covers slither to the ground!

Mouse, Kanga, Ben and Bella
on the big bouncy bed.

Boing!
Boing! Boing!
BOING! MIND YOUR HEAD!

Feathers flying everywhere,

bouncy bed jumps in the air!

But someone's peeping round the door . . .

"... Hi there, kids, is there room for more?"

"Course there is, Tiger. Come up and jump."
Tiger springs and the bed goes bump!

BUMP, bump, bumpety-bump!

Tiger and Mouse, Kanga, Bella and Ben
on the big bouncy bed,
bouncing high and then . . .

. . . in run Zebra, Dog and Duck.

Kangaroo is panic-struck!

And . . .

...into the room Elephant charges.

"**NO!**" they cry as Elephant barges . . .

. . . under the bed

hoisting it **high!**

Out through the window . . .

Then she flaps her ears
and up she flies!
On to the **big bed**, **soaring high**,

Up, up, up

to the starry sky.

Vroom! The bed zooms through the night.
"Everybody hold on tight!
Look at the planets! Look at the stars!

Look at Mercury!

Look at Mars!

Look at Saturn
and the Moon!

There's Jupiter

and there's Neptune!"

"Wow!" cries Bella. "This is ace!
We're whizzing round in outer space!"

"There's planet Venus. Let's land!" yells Ben.

"Too hot!" cries Bella.

"Pluto, then?"

"No, that's too cold,
and there's not enough light.

But that planet there looks JUST right!"

Planet Earth is all aglow,
like a crystal ball in a magic show!

There's our country!

There's our town!

There's our house!

We're coming . . .

. . . down!
Down!
Down!
Down!

The bed goes **vroom!**

Right back in
to . . .

...Mum and Dad's room!

Dive under the covers.
Pretend to be asleep.

Time to sleep now,
home again.
"Goodnight, Bella.
Goodnight, Ben."